Tiny

THE CYCLING FOX

WRITTEN BY RICHARD CANTLE • ILLUSTRATED BY PIP CLAFFEY

By a tall tree, on a little island,

lived a sometimes nifty,

sometimes yawny,

little red fox, called Tiny.

He had a long
bushy tail.

Little pointy ears.

A cheeky grin.

And rode a bright
red bicycle.

Yes, that's right, Tiny was no ordinary fox . . .
He was, in fact, the only fox who ever lived
that could ride a bicycle.

He had become quite the celebrity on Green Island . . . Other foxes would come from miles around to see Tiny riding his little red bicycle.

RING! RING!

Every morning, without fail,
Tiny would go out cycling.

Up and down, up and down the lane, Tiny would go . . .
Grinning at all the onlookers, Tiny would shout,
"Good morning, everyone!",
and ring his bicycle bell loudly.

One morning, however, nobody saw Tiny out cycling.
Tiny's uncle, Bill, who lived next door to Tiny,
was very worried.

Uncle Bill knocked
on Tiny's front door.
Rat-a-tat-tat!
"Why are you not out
cycling today, Tiny?"
he asked.

"I can't find my bicycle," cried Tiny.
"I went to the shed this morning
and it was gone!"
Tiny felt very sad, and he didn't
know what to do.

"Don't worry, Tiny," said Uncle Bill. "We will find it. First we will call police officer Rose to report the missing bicycle."

"Then we will ask
everyone to help
us look for it."

Officer Rose came to
Tiny's house and wrote
down all the details
about his bicycle.

Then she inspected
the shed for clues.

Uncle Bill picked up the telephone and started calling all the islanders. "Everyone, Tiny's bicycle is missing," said Uncle Bill. "We need to help him find it."

The islanders hunted everywhere for Tiny's bicycle. From the north of the island to the south, and from the east to the west.

But there was no sign of the bicycle anywhere . . .

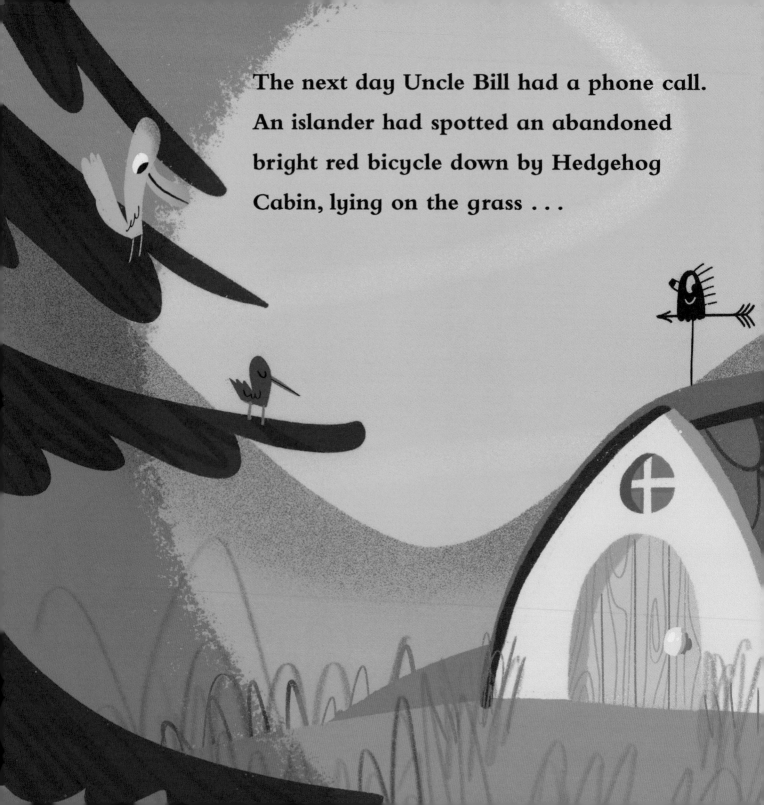

The next day Uncle Bill had a phone call.
An islander had spotted an abandoned
bright red bicycle down by Hedgehog
Cabin, lying on the grass . . .

As quick as could be, Uncle Bill
and Officer Rose were on their way.
It was indeed Tiny's bicycle!

Uncle Bill wheeled the bright red bicycle
all the way home to Tiny's house.
Rat-a-tat-tat!
"We've found your bicycle, Tiny!"
shouted Uncle Bill, knocking
on the door loudly.

"Thank you so much, Uncle Bill," said Tiny,

his trademark grin once again beaming across his face.

"I'm so happy and grateful to everyone for their help.

But who took my bicycle?"

"It was me," said Tiny's friend Sam,
as he stepped forward shyly.
"I just wanted to be like you . . .
I borrowed it, but I didn't know how
to ride it . . . I was going to return it,
but it was getting dark, and I ran out
of time to bring it back. I was too
embarrassed to tell you."

"Oh Sam, you should have told me.
Thank you for being brave
and admitting it."

The next morning Tiny was out on his bicycle again!

He wondered how he could thank everyone for searching for his bicycle.

"Aha! I know!" shouted Tiny
as he raced down the lane.
"I will offer cycling lessons
to all the other foxes on the island."

Very soon Tiny was not the only cycling fox
on Green Island . . .
Lots of foxes could now be seen cycling
around the island, grinning from ear to ear.

Tiny was so happy
that he could share
his love of cycling
with others.

The End

Printed in Great Britain
by Amazon